Mrs. Murphy's Crows

by Janice Boland
illustrated by Susan Hartung

Richard C. Owen Publishers, Inc.
Katonah, New York

Our teacher Mrs. Murphy feeds crows.
Every morning she scatters bread
on her window ledge and feeds the crows.

Then she comes to school.

One morning, Mrs. Murphy ran out of bread.

The crows were hungry!
They swooped from the rooftops.

They swooped from the trees.

They swooped down on Mrs. Murphy's head.

The crows followed Mrs. Murphy all the way
to school calling for their bread.

"CAW! CAW! CAW!"

The next day, we all brought bread to school.

We brought slices of bread and loaves of bread.

We brought breadsticks and biscuits, bagels and rolls.

We brought bags full of bread.

We brought armfuls and pocketfuls.

We gave it all to Mrs. Murphy.

Now Mrs. Murphy has bread for her crows.